KAFKA AT RUDOLF STEINER'S

Rosalind Palermo Stevenson

Rain Mountain Press
New York City

KAFKA AT RUDOLF STEINER'S

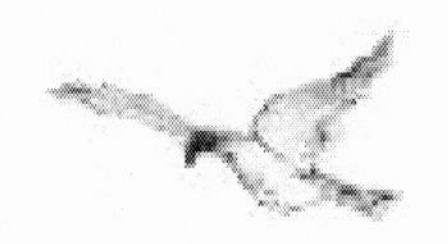

Rosalind Palermo Stevenson

ISBN: 978-0-9897051-9-6

KAFKA AT RUDOLF STEINER'S appeared in *First Intensity* (issue #21, Fall 2006)
and then in *Skidrow Penthouse* (issue #11, 2010). The author wishes to express
her grateful acknowledgement to these journals.

For all inquiries please contact info@rainmountainpress.com

Text set in New Aster
Designed by Sarah McElwain
First Edition

Printed in the United States of America

In memory of my grandfathers,
Angelo and Rocco

No, Mother, do not weep,

Most chaste Queen of Heaven

Support me always.

'Zdrowaś Mario' (*)

(Prayer inscribed on wall 3 of cell no. 3 of "Palace,"
the Gestapo's headquarters in Zakopane; beneath is the
signature of Helen Wanda Blazusiakowna, and the words,
"18 years old, imprisoned since 26, September, 1944.")

Henryk Gorecki's *Symphony No. 3.*
2nd movement: Lento E Largo – Tranquillissimo

(*) 'Zdrowaś Mario' (Ave Maria) – the opening of the Polish prayer to the Holy Mother

DUSK. The fading light. In a short while darkness. The grounds of the sanatorium. The building made of stone; the interior walls also stone, cool to the touch, on cold nights they feel like ice. Out of the shadows, W. Her hand.

Before leaving Prague, in Rudolf Steiner's chambers, I was faced with a dilemma: it was where to put the hat I had removed from my head. I clutched it in a gesture of nervousness. What is your interest in theosophy, Herr Kafka? Steiner asked me. (He will remain in Prague while he delivers his lectures on the subject of attainment of the spiritual worlds). I quickly cited my perplexity. I want to know the spiritual worlds, Herr Steiner, but I'm afraid it will add to the confusion of my life. My soul is split already between my life and my literary interest; I do what is expected outwardly, but inwardly the two are irreconcilable. I noticed a peg on the wall where I might hang my hat, but laid it instead on the wooden stand for lacing boots. Steiner's face: his expression grave, his brows knit together on his forehead.

Taking the waters now at Riva, the Christian girl, W, young, not yet twenty. She is here for treatment of her heart: weak heart activity and a murmur. Throughout the area the cold acidulous springs; the drinking cures: one liter every day. The sanatorium is a naturopathic establishment where I have come for ten days rest.

During lunch, I pass the pages of my story beneath the table to W. The story was written all night in a fury, until the sunrise, the sudden awareness of it becoming light outside the window. W's fingers touch mine then grab on to my story, a slight flush across her white skin. With one hand still beneath the table she is holding the manuscript, and with the other she pushes the food around on her plate. Then in polite conversation with the Russian woman who is sitting on her right. The excitement on W's face when she and the Russian woman turn full towards me to include me in their conversation.

The boats are sitting in a row outside the rowing house. Late at night I examine them again. The oars have been put up and sit stiffly at the bottoms of the boats. The smell of rain in the air, heavy, cool, tomorrow it will rain and we'll stay indoors. There will be the endless talk with the others about the condition of our bodies, the various ailments from which we suffer. Mine are digestive problems, dizziness, and inexplicable pains that travel through my body. W's smile today when I took her rowing. The calm surface of the lake as I rowed out from the shore, past the ledge which drops off; the lake is deep, just how deep I do not know; the water is black. A black abyss—perhaps three leagues down. An almost insuppressible urge to spring to my feet and leap headlong into the sombrous water. W, the way she smiled at me in the boat. She does not swim, yet was completely at ease in the rowboat.

I am delighted with the bathroom here, the large ornate mirror. The gradual understanding of my condition that seems to come from peering into it. The surface of the brass faucet is polished to a high finish. The water that runs from it has the faint smell of sulfur, a bitter taste each time I clean my teeth. In bed the question of my inability to sleep. The appearance of a ghostlike presence: a boy of nine or ten. He wears a cap, short pants, and a coat almost to his knees; on his face is the most desolate expression: terrible sorrowfulness; resignation and fear; his arms are raised in a gesture of surrender. I cannot see what enemy is menacing him, but all night long the boy remains; his arms are bent at the elbows and raised. W's face returns to my mind with the sunlight, the heavy top-drapes parted, the white, shear under-layer diffusing the light. Yesterday in W's eyes the look for a moment of worry, then changing to excitement.

It is a rarity for so many different springs to be found in a small area as is the case here; quite often one next to the other. Is your room to your liking, Herr Kafka? Your noon meal of parsnips and spinach as well? I am in a hydrotherapy tub in one of the treatment rooms, water from Ledro Spring is being pumped into the tub; my attention is fixed on the apparatus that controls the pumping. There is a bank of pipes along the yellowish wall; faucets and temperature gauges are attached to the pipes. The attendant adjusts the temperature of the water and prepares to leave the room. Herr Kafka, call out if you require my attention. Across from the hydro equipment is a cabinet that contains the basins for the inhalation therapy; dry gas packs that will be released into the basins.

A physical description of W: green eyes, brown hair with a reddish cast and a hint of curl. Her smile when she catches sight of me. One hand dangling over the side of the rowboat. The thin blue lines of her veins. Now, for this time, living completely influenced by W. Inexplicable calm. Followed by a rush of emotion.

The sun comes up. The long, slow lightening of the sky. The sky begins to grow light before the sunrise. On my bed, the stiff, white sheets. Does W sleep throughout the night untroubled? She has never mentioned sleeplessness. She told me she sleeps with my story, *The Judgment*, beneath her pillow. It is a disturbingly sad story, she told me.

Strange the way I'm thinking now of the male impersonator from the Yiddish troupe at the Cafe Savoy. Her enactment of the Wandering Jew. The long spread of her white collar, her hair covered by a hat. There is the song, too, that she sings. That moment when she comes onto the stage as a man. Her voice high-pitched in the style of the cantors. She wears men's short, black trousers, white stockings showing underneath. Her hands on her earlocks. Gooseflesh rising on my neck.

My dream repeats itself: just when it is coming to its conclusion, it returns to the beginning and starts again. I am on the grounds of the sanatorium. There is a thick growth of trees that covers the grounds. The smell of sulfur in the distance from the springs. A deep haze. The sky obscured by the thickness of the haze. I think, at first, they are vapors from the inhalation treatments. But then I realize they are fumes from burning. Ashes carried in the air, a smokestack rising in the shape of a funnel. It is a killing smoke, I shout in the dream. W suddenly appears beside me, she places her hand in mine.

Another water treatment at mid-day. The attendant standing in his white smock. I am immersed in the water and the quiet. A sudden intrusion: the sound of a barking dog. And a slight shock to my body when the water turns colder. In an instant it turns warm again. I am light-headed and tell the attendant, but he makes nothing of it. I am weightless in the water. My limbs as though floating detached from me.

Adam, where art thou? (Genesis). Rudolf Steiner and the Christian underpinning of his mysticism. God doesn't know where Adam is after the fall from light. Adam is gone. The sorrow, the grief of the spiritual world. These words in Steiner's writings: "Dreams rise up out of the ocean of unconsciousness." The word "dream" and I am instantly attentive. I have experienced the clairvoyant state that Steiner describes. I believe a dream I had last night was clairvoyant. The faces of my family rose before me staring straight ahead as in a detail from a painting, my mother and father prominent in the upper right. It was a wretched dream, suffused by helplessness, my mother's mournful face. My father wore dark glasses, the kind that blind men wear. My Uncle Alfred was situated to the left of my father; his head wrapped in dirty bandages. Positioned below my parents, were my sisters, pitiable. Ottla in her hat, a woman's fedora, a little tilted to one side; looking almost elegant except for her eyes: they were starkly open and gaping, the pupils reduced to pin-points as in a blazing light. And Valli and Elli next to Ottla, looking frightened and confused.

In the rowboat W tells me a secret, her face flushed, leaning a little forward towards me in the boat, I have never been in love before, she tells me. Her voice is unexpectedly husky. Excitement shows in her eyes. I continue rowing, the pull of the oars, the way the boat responds to the subtle shift in my attention to the oars. W looks, for a moment, as though she might stand and come sit next to me. Later in our rooms that are adjoined at top and bottom (hers is the one above) we communicate like children by knocking on the floor (her) and ceiling (me with a walking stick from my father's fancy-goods shop). The knocks are a wordless conversation. They start quite spontaneously, I knock first upon hearing her footsteps above me; I experience a kind of frenzy when I hear her footsteps, immediately followed by her answer.

The night of the comets. I prowl the grounds of the sanatorium. It will require an explanation when I try to re-enter the main house: the heavy bronzed door locked, a stern look on the face of the night attendant. Herr Kafka, he will say, what were you doing outside? Come in, come in, the night air will do no good for your condition. But Herr Attendant, I will say, my condition is that I've become a cat, like the strays in the alleyways in Prague. In the sky I see a streak of light, the comet's tail, the milky residue of stars, several flashes in immediate succession. I lie on the ground my face turned upward to the sky. Later, listening to W, in her room above mine; pacing.

Dreams, Steiner writes, are the guideposts to the invisible world, the world that exists parallel to the world of the senses. I think of my recurring dream of articles of clothing that fill the entire room. What do they mean running parallel to my life, all those shirts that dance in the air? With their stiffly starched collars the way my father's shirts are done at home. In my dream they are suspended in mid-air. The room is filled with shirts. All at once the sound of fluttering, like a bird—as though a bird has gotten into the room. W enters the dream dressed as a man like the male impersonator from the Yiddish troupe. Her hair is hidden beneath a hat, she wears men's trousers, the trousers come to just above the ankle. Beneath the trousers white stockings and small, pointed patent leather shoes. There is a photograph of Steiner on the cover of the book: his gaze is reflective (as though looking deeply inward) and ruminating (giving the impression he is taking everything into himself).

A contretemps tonight in the dining room, an awkward mix-up in the table assignments, in the seating arrangements at the tables. Those of us at the table are left feeling a little embarrassed. But then quickly everything is sorted out. Violins are part of the dinner entertainment. The lead violinist is a short man, balding. W sits across from me. She is like a schoolgirl tonight, alternately shy and excitable. A faint smile on her face while the introductions are being made for the entertainment. I smile too, one of those completely false smiles. The music is some kind of romantic air that holds W transfixed, her body leans towards mine. The desire to die in this moment, in its perfection.

Today the Russian woman tells fortunes with cards at the afternoon tea. When it is W's turn the fear of hearing her future drains all traces of color from her face. She is wearing a light blue chemise made out of a fabric that shimmers in the late noon sun. The Russian woman turns the cards over ceremoniously, in that way of fortune tellers. First the cards say that despite her illness, W is to live a long and comfortable life. And then the melancholy news that this life will nonetheless, be lived alone. I feel my heart beating wildly. I have already explained to W that we cannot continue beyond the days of our stay here at Riva—love bound to the physical is false love. I cannot live the life that would be required if W and I were to continue. And even if that were not true, what could we hope for? The gradual diminishment of love and of passion? The fate of everything that seeks to preserve itself in the world. W has acceded to this view. She has agreed that for our love to be preserved, we must let go of it. When our stay here has ended, there will be no visits, no letters, no pictures; we will not even speak each other's names. Yet now this pronouncement of the cards makes me feel forsaken.

The necessity of enduring life alone, and still the inability to bear it. Staring down at my fingers. A vague presentiment of the life that will be mine. And then recalling last night's dream: the appearance of Steiner, another visit to him, but this time a dream visit. The entrance to his study was dark, darker than it is in reality, and narrower too. There was an old woman in the dream; impossible to describe the effect she had on me. Pointing a finger in my direction. The old woman had also come to see Steiner, but she told me to go in ahead of her, to take all the time I needed, a tone of self-pity in her voice.

There is a chill in the air; we are drinking tea with lemon. I watch as W lifts the cup to her lips. The others sitting with us at the outdoor table are in animated conversation—the time spent in between the tubs and the treatments. We recognize that here we are our own community, although a strangely sad one. We live on and do not die from our complaints, but nonetheless we are separated from the lives of healthy people. The way my poor constitution—particularly my weak digestion which requires that I adhere to the most abstemious diet—has created an insurmountable barrier between myself and my family. My father is as strong as a lion. My mother and my sisters, too, are healthy. Especially my youngest sister, Ottla; despite her robust health I'm closest to her. How alike the two of us, Ottla and I. How impossible we find it to give ourselves over to human relationships. And yet the way our inability to do so defeats us. But now here, in this community, illness provides a common bond and the varied nature of the ailments is endless. Like the pain I feel this minute in my left shoulder.

Outside the window, branches threaten to break the glass, the wind of an approaching storm, the dark sky, W trembles, we have all come back inside and the conversation now continues in the salon, soon the dispersal of various parties to go to their rests, their treatments, their afternoon naps. Lingering with W, soon the room will be empty, the lake water violent, impossible to think we might go rowing. We watch like children out the window as the wind lashes at the trees. Thunder now, and lightning. W is pale in the dim light of the salon. I remain motionless.

The most important thing about death, Steiner writes, is what happens after; it is in the part that survives. Can we experience in life the state we will encounter after death? Yes, through one's clairvoyance it can be perceived while one is here. Steiner explores his subject in what he calls a scientific spiritual way: sound judgment and clear thinking must first be present, serious exercises and self-control; we cannot wait for clairvoyance to come to us like a dream. Nonetheless that is precisely the way my clairvoyance comes to me: in my dreams where I observe; innocent, abandoned as a child in the deepest darkness.

The intensification of my intimacy with W. Tonight I sat on the windowsill and called to her window above mine. She leaned out and we talked that way, softly, so as not to be heard by those in the adjoining rooms. Promises to steal away from the others tomorrow. Now in my bed with my heart beating too quickly. Lying on my back facing up towards the ceiling.

An encounter with the Russian fortune teller. She is without her cards, but I have no desire to know my future. Somewhat older, still attractive, reminds me of the actress in the Yiddish troupe, Mella Mars at the Cabaret Lucerna. Mella Mars, one of the great tragediennes. Her death scene makes us weak. Each night she dies for the man she loves, and we men in the audience substitute ourselves for the man who has caused her heartbreak. The Russian woman has that same theatrical air, deeply sensual, playful in the way that comes after the dependencies of youth. Intimation of the fulfillment of a dream: to be completely in such a woman's hands. But all possibility of its realization given up (gladly, without thought) for W.

In my mind these images of W: a single transparent hand, her green eyes intent on watching me. Her hand moves as if to touch me; it disappears, then it appears again and reaches for my face. In the distance W appears for real, the light behind her, dressed in white. As she approaches I can see her smile. She walks as if floating. She draws nearer. Love with W fully realized.

It is not we who see the dead. (Steiner writing on the subject of the presence of the dead.) The dead see us. We can only feel ourselves to be perceived by them. To be accurate, Steiner tells us, it must be stated this way: we experience the being of the dead and can feel it.

W wearing a hat to keep the sun off her face, the wide brim casts a shadow. She is quiet today, all my attempts at humor fail, but she touches my hand and asks to go rowing. On the lake, weeds grow along the shoreline. The middle is deep; it is boasted how deep, there is the ledge, which drops off, the sign with a warning to swimmers.

W drags her hand in the lake water as we push off from shore. She confesses she is afraid of water, of drowning. In the distance one of the nurses is walking along the shoreline. The boat tilts a little to one side. W grabs on to the boat and then regains her composure. We are still on the ledge; I can feel the bottom with my oar.

A brief spell of dizziness while telling W about the study of San Sebastian that I posed naked for as a favor to the artist, Ascher. I tell her perhaps to see her cheeks flush, which they do, with excitement and at the same time with embarrassment. The dizziness increases and I put my head down, W asks what the matter is, I say it is nothing and raise my head up. She does not believe it is nothing and insists we go inside. It is almost time for her treatment. Hers will be the hydrotherapy. Mine is something else, electrical stimulation to the extremities, both the hands and feet.

The red-cheeked nurse attending me (a woman) pulls at my feet and toes as she applies the little pads, and then the nodes of the electrical wires. Her attention to her work; she is all efficiency, moving briskly back and forth between me, on my back on the narrow bed with my naked legs and feet stretched out before me, and the sterile-looking white counter with the electricity cabinet hanging above it. She fiddles with the electrical controls. Are you quite comfortable, Herr Kafka? A few precise calculations and the machine starts to hum. I stare at the wires that hang out from the cabinet, encased in their pale, orange-colored tubing. The dials and gauges for measuring the current. What would happen, Frau Attendant, if too much current were to be directed through the wires? You would go poof in smoke, Herr Kafka. But at von Hartungen we know how to control the flow of the current. A surge of optimism brought about by thoughts of W. I am barely aware of the electrical manipulations to my feet.

The emphasis Steiner places on the ether body. The ether body, he maintains, is the subtle body between the mortal body and the soul. In death our entire life is retained in the ether body. I close my eyes. In the death I see there are only devastated landscapes; the sound of crying out as at the moment of dying; and then the great long sobs of the living.

The day of parting drawing near. W pale at breakfast this morning. She tells me she is worried about so many things—that out of her sight I will forget her; that she will not be able to live the life that follows when I am gone. She puts these worries before me without a trace of recrimination. The only happy thought she has, she tells me, is that the fortune teller shall prove correct, that she will live her life alone if it must be without me. In the afternoon we go rowing. W describes the effect that the water has on her, in the middle of the lake, so deep and at the bottom darkness. Is that a place we might exist? She asks. The purity of her emotion, the delicacy of her arms in the sleeveless shift when the shawl falls away. And I, in my role of the practiced rower, staring straight ahead at W. The strain of the oars as I row. W continues to gaze into the water, her shawl in folds on the seat of the rowboat. The desire to let my cheek come to rest against hers, or in that place above her shoulder, just below her chin. One of W's bare arms dangles over the side of the boat, I have put the oars up so that we can drift, we are the only boaters on the lake, drifting; imperceptible movement of the current of the lake.

In the evening an entertainment, this time a burlesque, similar to those performed in the small cafes in Prague. The actors enter, an initial note of uncertainty, the bright lights harsh on their faces. There are two actors, a man and woman, curiosity as to what will follow. W is seated next to me. Professor G on her right. The Russian woman, tonight a table away; she winked at me when I took my seat next to W. W doesn't laugh, not even at the most farcical jests of the actors. There is a moment during the entertainment when she bends towards me and whispers something. I cannot hear because of the laughter of the audience. W thinks that I have heard what she has said, smiles a small conspiratorial smile, meets my eyes with hers, seems especially satisfied, turns away from me and back to the stage, the slightest brushing of my wrist with her fingers. I speak W's name. She turns towards me and leans closer. I take note of the abandon in her gesture. She seems not to care who sees us. I speak her name again, more softly this time; she looks away and stares at her hands on the table in front of her.

Now in our respective rooms, knocks, footsteps, more knocks, more footsteps, then sitting on the window ledge, some childish calling up, ribbons lowered from her to me, the fear of waking the others, my exhaustion, I follow every movement she makes in her room, my body tense, resisting sleep as is my habit, a chill in the air, chilling my room through the open window, the pattern of knocks a language of its own, like a series of spoken words, but a language that cannot be translated,

I hear W as she walks across the room, other sounds as though objects are being moved, soon quieting down, I stare up at the ceiling and then close my eyes.

Disturbing dream of the brothel. The Madame appears without a smile, she is a stocky woman dressed in black. I have come with Max, Oscar B, and Ernst. The front parlor with the shutters lowered, a little musty but everything well-ordered. The whores parade in, scantily dressed in their work clothes. The first awkward moments, a sense of timidity, my impulse to leave. Ernst pushes me forward, Max and Oscar B are grinning. There is the odor of talc and perfume. One of the women stares at me (her hair flat against her head). And then the sudden shock of seeing W. She is standing towards the rear among the whores. Her child-face is painted and she is half-clothed in a transparent shift through which I can see her entire body. She looks at me uncomprehendingly, without recognition and yet it is clear to me has forgotten nothing, not even when Ernst, who is wheezing, leads her off to one of the rooms.

When I wake, I'm afraid: the knowledge of my life, of what it must be.

Overheard this morning on the way to the treatment room. "Herr Doktor, I seek to know more about the condition of my disease. I have eaten nothing but eggs for a week and still not the slightest improvement." Later, after my treatment, taking photographs with the others for Irene Bugsch's scrapbook. The photographs were taken outdoors against a stand of trees, behind us the mountain peaks, the sky clear, blue, small billows of haze hovering over the peaks. W was not part of the picture taking. The usual posing, herding together to fit inside the frame, everyone staring impassively, Irene Bugsch with her hand on her hip.

Afterwards resting. In my room again reading Steiner. We must immerse ourselves in the otherness, Steiner tells us; a few drawings scattered throughout the book, primitive illustrations that resemble my own stick-figure drawings. The book is an examination of the development of human consciousness: Steiner leading us to the precipice where we are to take the next leap forward and enter fully into the higher state of consciousness. Already I have the sense of the gathering darkness despite the fact it's early in the day. Everyone in a solemn mood at the sanatorium because of the death of the patient, Shauder. They have aired out his room. The airing out of death; that is, the attempt to bring air into the place death has been. Entering the treatment room this morning, I experienced this vision; the vision ran parallel to my actual entrance into the room: first a menacing chamber at the end of a path banked with stones; it was a long, narrow path which led to the chamber's rectangular black opening. On the other side, inexorable night, bottomless and unforgiving. I hear W singing now, in her room above mine, always unexpected the huskiness of her voice.

It is the day before W's departure. Her tears when we are alone out by the rowing dock. Brilliant sunlight, unimaginable sadness. And yet the effect of excitement. We walk around the grounds instead of rowing. W apologizing for her tears. She tells me it is as if a sentence of death has been handed down to us, irrevocable. She weeps uncontrollably. I take her hand to calm her. Remember all that we've promised, I tell her; our vow to share a perfect love: our love exists no matter where we are, fully realized outside the material world; it is timeless and beyond the reach of life and death. W looks up at me and responds: It has been ordained by the Russian fortune teller, her cards. She becomes more composed now; there is much discussion of the greatness of our love.

The old man is sitting under an umbrella, his face in profile, drooping chin and shoulders; he has come fresh from the baths with his skin still pink; I'm amazed at the way he is able to sleep in the open in the daylight. Inside my head a thundering scream. But detached, without cause; that is, without a cause I can apprehend. The sun is shining; it is very warm now. I stand with my arms folded in front of me.

The scheduled departure of W in the afternoon, imminent, certain. She has not yet come down from her room. Earlier this morning the sound of her footsteps. From five o'clock I lay awake listening. Now the others trail by on their way to the treatment rooms. I have canceled mine pleading dizziness, too light-headed today for the tubs. Eager for W's appearance, anxious, dreading that moment of parting which must come. I have done nothing all morning but watch for her, yet when she appears she takes me by surprise. She is already dressed in her traveling clothes, a gray silk jacket over her skirt and blouse, and a hat that is charming. The hat has a veil, which she has not pulled down over her face. There is time for one last walk, the woods damp from a heavy rain in the middle of the night, the smell of earth, everything damp under foot. W expresses some concern about her shoes, yet is insistent we continue walking. Her delicate, narrow face, the open expression, that way she has of staring directly at me.

In the woods with the sun breaking through and shining midst the branches of the trees. W's face lit by the sun. Her eyes shielded by one hand, the other I take in mine. A solemn oath to love always.

Walking back through the woods to the main house of the sanatorium. The smell of the wet earth reminds me of death—into the earth that will receive us. The way the graves will open at the last judgment. Bodies sitting up in amazement. We will know who we are then. My foreboding of a malevolent future lately rips continually at me. Hands stretch out before me, the hands of those lost to me and to the world; a woman's face; behind her, others. W's luggage has already been brought down. Her family has arrived to accompany her home.

Her family sits at the table at lunch. I am with them as a stranger. As one who has no real place among them. As one who longs for a real place among them. W stares at the food on her plate, pushes it around, lifts the fork to her lips but does not eat. Twice her eyes fill up with tears, but she does not let them fall. I wonder does her family notice. Her father is in conversation with Professor G. The latter's usual appetite, huge, voracious. Her father does most of the talking in a steady stream of words, occasionally directing some of them at me, I nod, perhaps inappropriately, too distracted to comprehend what he is saying. W's mother smiling. The family will depart after lunch, taking W with them.

And I, always the clown, it falls to me to prevent W from breaking into tears and weeping openly in front of her family. My limpid jokes amuse her, amuse the entire family, especially W's younger sister who is beginning to form an attachment to me. W's green eyes. Her mother's attention to her. Commenting on the progress her daughter has made with her health. Her mother has the same green eyes as W. W is like a child with her mother. I imagine, for a moment, that I, too, am that woman's child, and in that way of the same blood as W. W perhaps reads my thoughts, the flush on her cheeks, the high color.

And then the walk down to the landing pier where the family will board the steamer. The women in the farewell party embrace W. Vigorous shaking by the men of her father's hand. W's eyes remain fixed on me.

W at the rail of the steamer.

Some silly frantic waving by her younger sister. The steamer pushes off. Watching until the boat is out of sight.

To be reminded now of W continually.

On my return to Prague, I again visit Steiner; I put the question to him: what remains? What remains of one's experience? What will remain? Steiner's usual grave expression. That way he has of not answering a question. My hat sitting again on the stand for lacing boots. If I could have continued with W beyond the ten days at Riva there might have been some chance for me. I have dramatized it in my mind as my last chance. And still the question what will remain? Of what has been. Of what will be. Mella Mars at the Cabaret Lucerna. Madame X, the male impersonator in the Yiddish troupe. Max on his wedding night, the excitement of the brothels. My father in the end helpless in his nightshirt. My mother whose only wish was to keep me alive. And my sister Ottla in her tiny row house behind Hradžany Castle. Franz, she said, come Franzie, I have found the nicest house for you to live in. It is small, but it will suit your needs. It is one of the row houses that belong to the Castle. And then the pity of Ottla at Auschwitz. Where she will die. Where Valli and Elli will also die—but before that will be my own death. And before that will be my last dream. A ridiculous and meaningless dream. It will be of shirts, a strange sight to see them. Shirts of the kind I used to wear. Floating all around me in the room. What do they mean? *Too late. The sweetness of sorrow and of love. To be smiled at by her in the boat. That was the most beautiful of all. Always only the desire to die and the not-yet-yielding; this alone is love.*

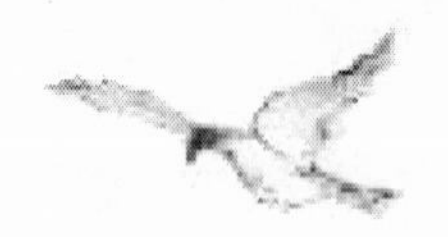

NOTES

Kafka At Rudolf Steiner's

In March, 1911, the mystical philosopher, Rudolf Steiner, delivered a series of lectures in Prague on the subject of *An Occult Physiology,* which included, among others, the subjects: The System of Supersensible Forces; The Blood as Manifestation and Instrument of the Human Ego; The Conscious Life of Man; and, The Human Form and its Co-ordination of Forces.

In *The Diaries of Franz Kafka, 1910–1913* (translated by Joseph Kresh and edited by Max Brod), Kafka mentions attending the Rudolf Steiner lectures in Prague on the evenings of March 26, 1911 and March 28, 1911. The diary entry for March 28, 2011 contains an entry which Kafka titled: My Visit To Dr. Steiner. This entry describes his visit to and impressions of Dr. Steiner.

Between late September and early October 1913, Kafka entered the von Hartungen sanatorium in Riva, where he met and fell in love with the young girl referred to in the story as W, and believed by some Kafka scholars to be Gerti Wasner. The diary entry for October 15, 1911 *(The Diaries of Franz Kafka, 1910–1913)* contains this reference to the girl: *"The stay in Riva was very important to me. For the first time I understood a Christian girl and lived almost entirely within the sphere of her influence. I am incapable of writing down the important things that I need to remember."*

In 1914 Kafka writes a letter of confession about the Christian girl to his fiancé, Felice Bauer, telling her how much the young girl meant to him and that on their parting [from Riva] they had to hold back tears.

Kafka's sisters, along with their families, were sent to the Łódź Ghetto in Poland and either died there, or in concentration camps. Ottla is believed to have died in the death camp at Auschwitz.

The last five lines of the story (italicized) are a direct quote from *The Diaries of Franz Kafka,* 1910–1913, entry dated October 22, 2013.

Cover Art

The cover art is a detail of *Königsgraben*, a drawing on the ceiling of the penal colony barrack at Birkenau. A sign in the barrack gives the following details. "A special penal company *(Strafkompanie)* for men was housed in this barrack from May 1942 to July 1943. These were mainly political prisoners, people for some reason considered particularly dangerous to the Third Reich, prisoners found guilty of breaking camp discipline, or those who were thought to be participating in the camp's underground movement or planning to escape. They were kept in complete isolation from the other prisoners; even the daily roll-call and distribution of rations were done separately in an enclosed yard next to the barrack. Conditions in this unit were extremely harsh. Punishments were severe, the workload murderous, and food rations reduced—all leading to high mortality rate. One of the tasks of this unit was to dig the main drainage ditch (Königsgraben). An original drawing of this made by an unknown prisoner still remains on the ceiling of this barrack."